W9-BHI-689

A DARK DARK TALE

For William, Edward and Alice Cowling

First published in the United States 1981
by Dial Books for Young Readers
A Division of Penguin Books USA Inc.
375 Hudson Street
New York, New York 10014

Published in Great Britain
by Andersen Press Ltd.
Copyright © 1981 by Ruth Brown
Library of Congress Catalog Card Number: 81-66798
First Pied Piper Printing 1984
Printed in the U.S.A.
COBE
40 41 42 43 44 45 46 47 48 49
A Pied Piper Book is a registered trademark of
Dial Books for Young Readers,
a member of Penguin Putnam Inc.
® TM 1,163,686 and ® TM 1,054,312.

A DARK DARK TALE
is published in a hardcover edition by
Dial Books for Young Readers.
ISBN 0-14-054621-9

The art consists of acrylic paintings that are
color-separated and reproduced in full color.

A DARK
DARK TALE

Story and pictures by

RUTH BROWN

PUFFIN BOOKS

Once upon a time there was a dark, dark moor.

On the moor there was
a dark, dark wood.

In the wood there was
a dark, dark house.

At the front of the house
there was a dark, dark door.

**Behind the door there
was a dark, dark hall.**

In the hall there were
some dark, dark stairs.

Up the stairs there was dark, dark passage.

Across the passage was
a dark, dark curtain.

Behind the curtain was
a dark, dark room.

In the room was a dark,
dark cupboard.

In the cupboard was
a dark, dark corner.

In the corner was
a dark, dark box.

And in the box there was . . . A MOUSE!

RUTH BROWN

studied art at the Birmingham College of Art and the Royal College of Art. She has worked on animated films for the BBC and is the author of one previous children's book, *Crazy Charlie.*

Ms. Brown lives in London with her husband and two sons.